Snug in the Tent

Written by Suzy Senior

Illustrated by Erin Brown

Collins

I like to camp in a tent.

It's best when it rains. I feel snug.

Now, there is just far too much rain.

Splish! Splash! Splosh!
Will this rain ever stop?

I see lots of droplets on the tent.

I hear them drip.

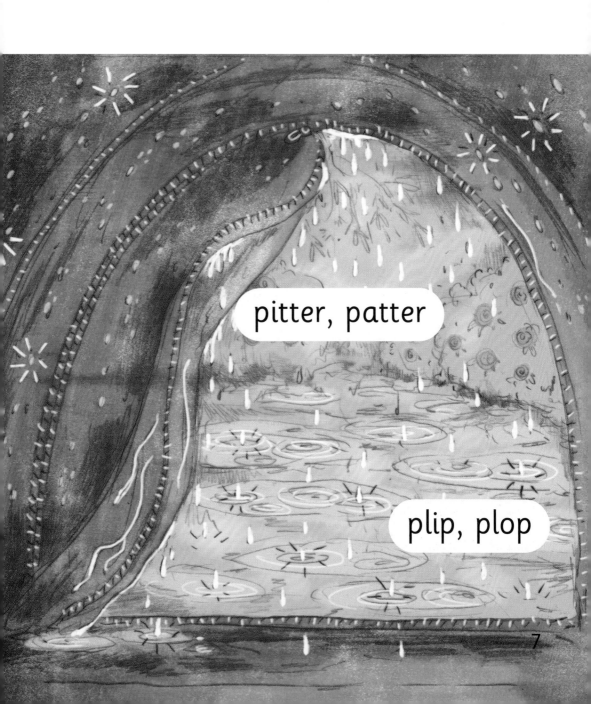

pitter, patter

plip, plop

Splat! Now the rain lands in the tent.

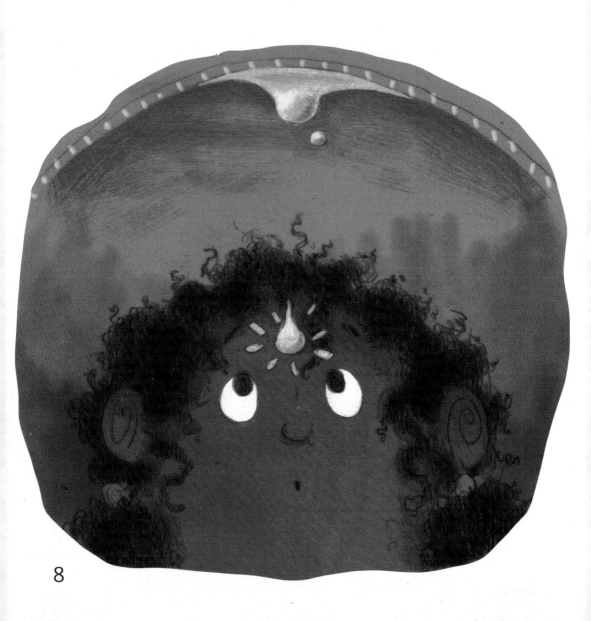

Drips splash into my rucksack.
My blanket gets damp.

Gran yells, "It's too wet for tents. Come in!"

I grab my stuff and sprint back in.

I can still camp in my bedroom.